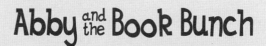

Abby and the Book Bunch

THE MYSTERY OF THE GOLDEN KEY

by Nancy K. Wallace

illustrated by Amanda Chronister

magic wagon

visit us at www.abdopublishing.com

For my husband, Dennie, and my original Book Bunch: Hanna, Derrick, & Dakota —NW

Published by Magic Wagon, a division of the ABDO Group, PO Box 398166, Minneapolis, MN 55439. Copyright © 2013 by Abdo Consulting Group, Inc. International copyrights reserved in all countries. All rights reserved. No part of this book may be reproduced in any form without written permission from the publisher.

Calico Chapter Books™ is a trademark and logo of Magic Wagon.

Printed in the United States of America, North Mankato, Minnesota.
102012
012013

 This book contains at least 10% recycled materials.

Text by Nancy K. Wallace
Illustrations by Amanda Chronister
Edited by Stephanie Hedlund and Rochelle Baltzer
Layout and design by Neil Klinepier

Library of Congress Cataloging-in-Publication Data
Wallace, Nancy K.
  The mystery of the golden key / by Nancy K. Wallace ; illustrated by Amanda Chronister.
     p. cm. -- (Abby and the Book Bunch)
  Summary: Puzzled over what to write for a creative writing contest, Abby finds inspiration when her dog digs up an old key on a gold chain and she sets out, with the help of Mrs. Mackenzie the public librarian, to solve the mystery of the golden key.
  ISBN 978-1-61641-915-8
1. Locks and keys--Juvenile fiction. 2. Public libraries--Juvenile fiction. 3. Books and reading--Juvenile fiction. 4. Creative writing--Juvenile fiction. [1. Locks and keys--Fiction. 2. Public libraries--Fiction. 3. Books and readings--Fiction. 4. Creative writing--Fiction. 5. Mystery and detective stories.] I. Chronister, Amanda, ill. II. Title.
  PZ7.W158752Mys 2013
  813.6--dc23
                                              2012027943

CONTENTS

A Dog's Life

"Spring break," Dakota sighed. He stretched out on Abby Spencer's front porch. He stared at the blue sky and smiled. "No school for seven days! I love it!"

Abby headed for the porch swing. She sat down and tucked one foot under her. "We only have two weeks until the library's creative writing contest," she said. "I haven't written a thing yet!"

"Neither have I!" Sydney groaned, flopping down beside her. The swing swayed gently back and forth. "I was so excited when I signed up. Now, I don't even have any ideas. Who knew it was so hard to write a book!"

"It doesn't have to be very long," Abby told her. "Mrs. Mackenzie said we could write a short story."

Mrs. Mackenzie was the children's librarian at Evergreen Library. Abby and her friends liked to help at the library after school. Mrs. Mackenzie always found fun things for them to do. She called them Abby and the Book Bunch because they spent so much time helping at the library!

Dakota raised his head. "Here's a short story for you," he said. "'The dog ate my homework.' You could write that in really big letters. It might take up a whole page!"

Abby giggled. Her golden retriever,

Lucy, was digging a hole in the yard. She was halfway under a bush. Dirt shot into the air. Lucy was showering the yard with earth and stones.

"Lucy *did* eat my homework once," Abby said. "I didn't think Mr. Kim would believe me when I told him. But he had met Lucy at the school festival last fall. He said he wasn't surprised."

Sydney laughed. "Everyone knows that Lucy eats all kinds of stuff!"

Abby sighed. "She chewed up my dad's favorite ball cap yesterday," she said.

Sydney nodded. "He told me this morning when I came over. She ate one of my shoelaces last week."

"She ate my free cheeseburger coupon, too!" Dakota added. "It was just like she stole food right out of my mouth!"

Sydney pointed at Dakota. "Give us a break! Abby's dad bought you a cheeseburger!" she reminded him. "So you still got a free one."

"I was just saying that she ate my coupon," Dakota grumbled. He stood up and grabbed a red ball off the porch. "I really wish I had a dog." He threw the ball high in the air. "Catch, Lucy!"

Lucy wheeled around. Her tail wagged frantically. Her nose and paws were covered with dirt. She leaped through the air and caught the ball in her mouth.

"Good girl!" said Dakota. "Now bring it here."

Lucy ran back toward the bushes where she had been digging. She dropped the ball in the hole. Her paws threw dirt in all directions. She quickly covered up the ball.

"Oh man, she's burying it!" Dakota groaned. He ran down the steps to rescue the ball.

Abby pushed the swing with one foot. "Maybe I'll write a story about a princess for the contest," she said.

Sydney frowned. "Katie already wrote one about a princess. She finds a magic ring or something."

"I could write about a caterpillar that becomes a beautiful butterfly," Abby suggested.

"Zachary's writing one like that," Sydney replied.

Abby stopped swinging. "Zachary's writing about a butterfly?" she asked in surprise.

"Well, it's a soldier caterpillar. It turns into a butterfly with bombs and missiles," Sydney explained.

Abby rolled her eyes. "That sounds more like Zachary."

"Hey, Abby," Dakota called from the front yard, "come see what Lucy found!"

Abby looked at Sydney. They both ran down the steps and across the yard.

Dakota was kneeling down. He peered into the hole that Lucy had dug. He held the red ball clutched in one hand. His finger pointed to an object half covered in dirt. "What do you think that is?" he asked.

Buried Treasure

Dakota gently brushed dirt away from the bottom of the hole. "It's some kind of chain," he said.

"It looks like a necklace," said Sydney.

"Maybe it's gold," whispered Abby.

Dakota broke a branch off a bush. "I'll dig it out with this stick!"

"Be careful," warned Sydney. "It might be old. You should let Abby do it. It's her yard."

"I found it!" Dakota protested.

"Lucy found it," Sydney reminded him. "And Lucy is Abby's dog. Whatever she found belongs to Abby."

Dakota sighed and sat back on his heels. "All right," he said. "But I think it should be mine, too."

Abby ran a finger over the chain. "I don't know how to get it out," she said. "I don't want to break it."

Dakota held out the stick. "Use this," he offered.

Abby pushed the stick into the ground next to the chain. The dirt crumbled away. A little more of the chain came out of the dirt. Abby moved it carefully to the side. She pushed the stick into the dirt again.

Lucy dropped her ball into the hole. "No, Lucy," said Abby. "You can't help."

Lucy wagged her tail and smiled.

"Sit, Lucy," said Dakota.

Lucy lay down in the hole. She rolled over and showed them her tummy.

Sydney tried to push her away. "Move, Lucy!" she yelled.

"Here, Lucy," said Dakota. "Get the ball." He sent the red ball flying across the yard.

Lucy ran after it. Her tail floated out behind her like a flag.

"Hurry," Sydney told Abby. "She will come right back."

Abby bent over the hole. "I'm working as fast as I can," she said. She twisted the stick back and forth. Dirt fell away from the chain. It was almost free.

Abby could see something was attached to the chain. There was a loop of metal and something else, too.

Lucy ran back. She dropped the ball in the hole and sat down. She was panting. Her tongue hung out of her mouth. She slobbered into the hole.

Abby grabbed the ball. She shoved it at Dakota. "Throw it again," she said.

Dakota pitched the ball as far as he could. Lucy jumped up and raced away. Dakota dropped down on his knees by Abby. "Hurry up!" he begged.

Abby slipped her hands back into the hole. She rubbed frantically at the shape in the dirt. She tugged gently on the chain. It pulled free!

"It's a key!" she cried.

Dakota leaned closer to see. Sydney knelt down next to him.

"Oh, look! It's really old," Sydney said.

The key was long and narrow. The top of it was packed with dirt.

"Let's clean it off," said Abby. They ran over to the porch steps. Abby got the hose and sprayed it gently. Then, she rubbed it on her shirt to dry it. The key glittered in the sunlight.

"It's beautiful," Sydney said. "Look, it has your initial on it!"

The top of the key formed a heart with the letter "A" in the center.

Abby touched the letter with her finger. "A," she said. "For Abby."

Dakota jumped up and down. "Maybe it's Captain Ahab's. Maybe it's the key to a treasure chest!" he cried.

"There weren't any pirates in Evergreen, Dakota!" said Sydney. "It's probably just an old necklace. Maybe it had the first letter of someone's name."

Abby didn't answer. She carefully slipped the chain over her head. There was something very special about this key. She was sure of it. And now it belonged to her.

The Key to a Mystery

Abby, Dakota, and Sydney ran inside. Lucy bounded after them. Lucy's tail wagged back and forth. Abby's mom and dad were drinking coffee at the kitchen table.

Abby laid the key gently on the table. "Look what Lucy dug up in the yard," she said.

"Oh my!" said Abby's mom. "I'll bet that chain is gold!"

"Do you think so?" Abby asked. "The key has my initial on it."

Her dad held the key up to the light. "The key is probably made of brass," he said. "Gold is a soft metal. A key made of gold would bend too easily."

Abby wished the key was made of gold. That seemed more magical. "It's still pretty," she said.

"It's very pretty," her mom agreed.

"See the little marks on the end of the key?" Abby's dad asked. "This key has been used. So, it wasn't just a necklace."

"I wonder what it opened," Abby said.

Dakota bounced up and down excitedly. "Maybe there is a treasure chest!" he suggested. "We should get a shovel and make the hole bigger."

"Where did you find it?" Abby's dad asked.

"Under the bushes by the sidewalk," Abby said.

"It looks like a house key," said Abby's dad. "But it's not the key to this house. Our house was built in 1940. This key looks much older than that."

"How could we find out more about it?" Abby asked.

"Why don't you ask Mrs. Mackenzie?" said Abby's dad. "Maybe she has some information about old keys."

Abby clapped with excitement. "Can you walk us to the library?" she asked.

Abby's dad stood up. "I'll drive you," he said. "I need to get some things at the hardware store. I want to tear down that old shed behind the garage next week."

"Awesome!" said Dakota. "Can I help? I love to tear stuff down."

"We'll see," said Abby's dad. "I don't want you to get hurt."

Dakota bent his arms to show his muscles. "I'm very strong."

Abby's dad laughed. "I can see that," he said.

"I always liked that old shed," said Abby's mom. "The old door with the round top is so cute! And I love that flower that's carved in the middle of the door."

"It needs a new roof," said Abby's dad. "And the windows need to be replaced. It would cost a lot to fix it." He grinned at his wife. "I'll save the door."

Abby fingered the key in her hand. "Can I keep this?" she asked.

Abby's mom smiled. "I don't know why not," she said. "You found it."

"Dakota found it," Abby said.

"Lucy found it first," said Sydney.

"Well, it has your initial on it," said Abby's dad. "I think it should belong to you."

"Thanks," Abby whispered. She slipped the chain over her head. The key felt warm against her chest. She was so glad that it belonged to her!

"Now, if Lucy digs up a treasure chest," said Abby's dad, "I think we will all have to share."

"Cool!" said Dakota. He gave him a high five. "Can I dig out there this afternoon?"

"Maybe," said Abby's dad. "Let me see if you can do it without digging up the hedge."

"I'll be careful!" Dakota said.

"Would you like a sandwich before you go to the library?" Abby's mom asked.

"Yes!" said Dakota and Sydney at the same time.

Abby hesitated. She didn't want to take time to eat. She wanted to go to the library right away.

Abby's dad patted her shoulder. "I have to change anyway. You eat a sandwich. I'll be right down to take you to the library."

"Okay," said Abby. She helped her mom get plates out of the cupboard.

"Maybe we can get ideas for what to write for the contest while we're at the library," said Sydney.

"Maybe," said Abby. She touched the chain around her neck. Suddenly, the contest didn't seem so important. Abby just wanted to find out more about her key.

Lollipops and Dragons

People were gathered on the sidewalk outside Evergreen Library. Two ladies sat on a bench reading in the warm spring sunshine. Kids and parents were going in and out of the doors. Abby, Dakota, and Sydney passed Katie by the circulation desk.

"Hi!" said Abby and Sydney.

"Hi!" said Katie. She pointed at her big stack of books. "I got some extra books to read over vacation."

"I need to get more books, too," said Sydney.

Katie flicked her hair back. "Did you finish your story for the contest?" Katie asked.

"No," said Sydney.

"No," said Abby and Dakota.

Katie smiled and giggled. "I just gave mine to Mrs. Mackenzie," she said. "I turned it in two weeks early!"

Abby looked at the floor.

Sydney smiled at Katie. "That's great," she said.

"My mom thinks I'll win. She says my story is very creative," Katie said. "And it's great to be done. Now I can enjoy my vacation!"

"Have a good time," Sydney said.

Abby waved as Katie walked out the door. Then, she turned to Sydney. "She's already done!" she hissed. "I haven't even started yet!"

Dakota shook his head. "Don't worry about it."

"She always turns everything in early," said Sydney. "I think she just wants to make everyone else look bad. We have two weeks left. We can still write great stories."

The Children's Area was packed with parents and kids. A toddler was climbing up the bookshelves while his mother picked out some books. Mrs. Mackenzie grabbed the little boy just as he started to crawl over the top.

"Good catch!" Dakota yelled.

Mrs. Mackenzie put the toddler on the floor. He waddled off with a red lollipop stuck to the back of his pants. A little girl jumped off the window seat into a pile of floor pillows. The toy train clattered into sight loaded with blocks. A girl with an engineer's hat was yelling, "Toot! Toot!"

Mrs. Mackenzie wiped her forehead. "It's crazy in here today," she said.

Two first grade boys were fighting over the dragon. Both of them were trying to ride it at the same time.

Mrs. Mackenzie grabbed one boy in each hand. "Why don't you take turns?" she suggested quietly. "Each of you can sit on the dragon for three minutes." She held up her watch. "I'll time you."

"I go first!" snapped one boy. He pushed the other boy away and climbed on. The second boy screamed and started to cry.

Mrs. Mackenzie patted him. "It will be your turn next, Isaac," she said. She turned to Abby, Dakota, and Sydney. "Are you having fun on your break?"

They all nodded. "We found something awesome in Abby's front yard," Dakota said. "Lucy dug it up! Show it to her, Abby."

Abby slipped the necklace over her head. She handed it to Mrs. Mackenzie.

"This is a beautiful key!" said Mrs. Mackenzie. "Did you put it on the chain, Abby?"

Abby shook her head. "No, it was on the chain when we found it."

"So it was a necklace?" Mrs. Mackenzie asked.

"My dad said the key has been used," said Abby. "So we think it opened something."

"We just don't know what it opened," said Sydney.

Mrs. Mackenzie turned the key over in her hand. "Well, it's too big for a jewelry box key," she said.

"I think it's the key to a treasure chest!" said Dakota.

Mrs. Mackenzie laughed. "That would be nice, wouldn't it?" she said. "I think it looks more like a house key."

"My dad said the key isn't to our house," Abby said.

Mrs. Mackenzie frowned. "You found it in your yard. Maybe someone dropped it there. Or maybe it belonged to someone who used to live in your house."

"I wonder who used to live in my house before us," Abby said.

Mrs. Mackenzie smiled. "I know the people who lived in your house! Their names were James and Rachel Patterson. I think they built that house. They used to come to the library a lot when I first worked here."

"But the key has an *A* on it," Sydney said. "Patterson begins with a *P*."

"You're right, it does," said Mrs. Mackenzie. "James and Rachel don't begin with an *A* either. And they didn't have any children."

"My dad thought you might have some books on old keys," Abby said.

"I might," said Mrs. Mackenzie. "But I think we need to look at some other books first. Let's go over to the restricted section. I have an idea!"

Dakota gave Abby a high five. "I love the restricted section!" he said.

Mrs. Mackenzie looked at the floor. She held up her watch. "Three minutes!" she announced.

"Oh man," grumbled the little boy on the dragon.

Isaac pushed him off the dragon. "My turn!" he yelled.

Historic Discoveries

They passed the sign about the creative writing contest as they walked by the circulation desk.

"How are your stories coming?" asked Mrs. Mackenzie.

Abby sighed. "I haven't written anything yet."

"Dakota and I haven't either," said Sydney.

"Well, don't worry," said Mrs. Mackenzie. "You still have two weeks to write your stories. Katie is the only one who has turned hers in."

"She told us," said Sydney.

Mrs. Mackenzie laughed. "You don't sound very happy about it."

"She made us feel bad," said Abby. "She is all done and we haven't started yet."

Mrs. Mackenzie laughed again. "It doesn't matter who finishes first," she reminded her. "Whoever writes the best story will win!"

"Who is judging the contest?" asked Sydney.

"I asked Mr. Jackson to be the judge," said Mrs. Mackenzie. "He's an author who lives right here in Evergreen. He writes adult mystery novels."

"Mr. Jackson is my neighbor," said Abby.

Dakota wheeled to look at her. "That's not fair! If you know him, he might pick your story!"

Mrs. Mackenzie shook her head.

"Mr. Jackson won't know who wrote the stories," she explained. "I'm giving each story a number. I am the *only one* who knows which name goes with which number."

"I guess that's okay then," Dakota grumbled.

Mrs. Mackenzie reached the restricted section first. She slid the big library ladder over to the end of the bookshelves. "We have some books on the history of Evergreen," she said. "That's why we keep them back here. There is even one about old houses."

"Is my house in it?" Abby asked.

"Let's see," said Mrs. Mackenzie. She climbed up the ladder and took three books off the shelf. She climbed back down and put the books on a table.

The biggest book was called *Historic Houses of Evergreen*. Abby turned the pages carefully. Black and white pictures showed lots of different houses. Some had funny old cars in front of them. Some pictures showed people dressed in old-fashioned clothing.

"How would I find my house?" Abby asked.

"There's an index in the back. It lists the address and the owners of the houses," said Mrs. Mackenzie. "What's your address, Abby?"

"It's 549 Pine Street," said Abby.

Mrs. Mackenzie ran her finger down the index. "Here it is," she said. "Page forty-one has 549 Pine Street."

Abby's heart thumped while Mrs. Mackenzie turned the pages. Maybe she would find out the name of the person who owned her necklace!

Mrs. Mackenzie was shaking her head. "This must be a mistake," she said.

Sydney, Dakota, and Abby all leaned close to see. The house in the picture was huge! It had three floors. The big front porch covered the whole front of the house. The porch had carved wood on the posts and railings.

"It's beautiful," whispered Abby. "It looks like a wedding cake!"

"But it's not your house," said Sydney.

Dakota pointed under the picture. "It says 549 Pine Street," he said.

Mrs. Mackenzie frowned. "Maybe the name of the street has changed," she said. "Or maybe this book was written before your house was built!"

"I don't understand," said Abby.

Mrs. Mackenzie turned to the front page of the book. "This book was printed in 1938," she said. "Didn't your dad say your house was built in 1940?"

"Yes," said Abby. "But what happened to that great big house?"

"Maybe it tells us in this book," said Mrs. Mackenzie. She turned back to page forty-one.

Mrs. Mackenzie read out loud. "This beautiful old Victorian home was built by George and Mary Flynn in 1883. Flynn was one of the founders of the town of Evergreen."

"Wow!" said Dakota. "That was a long time ago!"

"Shhh!" said Abby. "Please read the rest, Mrs. Mackenzie."

"The house was destroyed by a fire in 1937," read Mrs. Mackenzie.

"It burned," gasped Sydney. "That's so sad. It was so beautiful!"

Abby held the key in her hand. She tried to keep the disappointment out of her voice. "It's not the right name, anyway," she said. "I was hoping that

someone whose name begins with an A owned it."

"Wait, there's more," said Mrs. Mackenzie. She began to read again.

"At the time of the fire, the home was owned by George Flynn's granddaughter, Abigail," read Mrs. Mackenzie. "Abigail Flynn sold the property after the fire. It was later divided into four smaller lots."

Abby was only thinking about one thing. "Her name was Abigail," she whispered. "That's my name. This key must have been hers."

"You have the same name," Sydney said in a hushed voice.

"Whoa!" said Dakota wiggling his eyebrows. "That's creepy!"

Unexpected News

When they got back from the library, Dakota helped Abby's dad carry some things to the garage. Abby and Sydney ran into the kitchen. Gram and Abby's mom were stacking newspapers to recycle. Abby spread out the pages she had copied at the library on the kitchen table.

"Look," she said, pointing. "We think the key must have belonged to Abigail Flynn! She owned this huge house. It used to be right here. She lived at 549 Pine Street, too!"

Abby's mom and Gram looked at the picture. "Oh my," said Abby's mom. "That house looks like a mansion!"

"Where did you find a picture of it?" asked Gram.

Abby danced from one foot to the other. "Mrs. Mackenzie has a book with pictures of old houses in it," she said. "Abigail's grandfather was George Flynn. He built this house in 1883!"

"I've heard of George Flynn," said Abby's mom. "He donated the money to build the first school in Evergreen. He was a very important man. The road that runs past the Evergreen Shopping Center is called George Flynn Highway."

Gram put on her glasses and studied the picture. "It's such a beautiful house," she said. "Why would they tear it down?"

"They didn't tear it down," said Abby. "The book said it burned a long time ago."

Gram shook her head. "What a shame!" she said.

"Lucy dug up a key under the front hedge this morning," Abby's mom explained. "The kids went to the library to see if they could find out how old it was." She smiled at Abby. "I guess you found out a lot more!"

Abby slipped the key off of the chain. She laid it in Gram's hand. "This key must have been Abigail Flynn's," said Abby. "It has her initial on it."

Gram frowned. "It's odd that she had her first initial on her house key," she said. "I would have thought it would be an F for Flynn."

"Maybe it was her own special key," said Abby.

"Maybe," said Gram.

Sydney looked out the window at the hedge. "Dakota wants to dig in your yard this afternoon, Mrs. Spencer," she said. "Is that okay?"

Abby's mom laughed. "Ask Abby's dad. He's out looking at the shed."

Abby grabbed her key. She ran out the back door with Sydney and Lucy at her heels. Her stomach felt like it was full of butterflies! Maybe something else from Abigail Flynn's house was buried in the yard! She wanted to dig, too!

Abby's dad held a ladder. Dakota was halfway up it peering at the shed roof. The shed looked old and sad. The shutters hung crookedly. Some of the small panes in the tall, thin windows were broken. Old yellow paint showed where the newer white paint had chipped away.

"I thought you wanted to dig under the hedge," said Abby.

Dakota hung on to the ladder with one hand and turned to look at her. The head of a hammer poked out of his pocket. "I can't," he explained. "I'm going to help your dad tear the shed down!"

Abby's dad shook his head. "We're not going to do it today, Dakota," he said. "I have to get a dumpster first to put all the wood in."

"We could start," Dakota coaxed.

"I have a meeting this afternoon," Abby's dad said. "Maybe we can work on it tomorrow."

"Oh man," Dakota complained. He slowly climbed down the ladder.

Abby could tell he was disappointed. "We can still look for old stuff under the hedges," she suggested. "Maybe we'll find something awesome!"

"Abby!" called Gram from the back porch. She was waving a newspaper. "Come here! You have to see this!"

Abby turned and ran back to the house. Lucy got there first. She jumped at the paper in Gram's hand.

Gram held the newspaper up so Abby could see it. "Look!" she said.

The headline read: "Area Resident Turns 100!" Below was a picture of a little old lady with white hair. She sat smiling in a wheelchair. A nurse held a birthday cake with lots of candles.

Abby frowned. "I don't understand," she said. "Who is this?"

"It's Abigail Flynn!" exclaimed Gram.

Abby felt as though her heart had stopped beating. "What?" she whispered.

Gram pointed to yesterday's date on the newspaper. "Look, Abby! Abigail Flynn is still alive. She lives at Evergreen Nursing Home!"

"Do you think it's the same Abigail Flynn?" Abby gasped.

"Well, there's only one way to find out," said Gram. "We could go and visit her! I could take you tomorrow morning."

"Oh, yes! Please take me, Gram," said Abby. "I want to meet her!"

Abby and Abigail

Abby's foot went *tap, tap, tap* against the floor of the car. Evergreen Nursing Home was just a few miles from Abby's house. But today it seemed like a hundred miles! Abby could hardly wait!

Gram stopped at a traffic light. She looked over at Abby and smiled. "We're almost there," she said.

"I was so excited that I could hardly sleep last night," said Abby.

"Did you and Sydney work on your stories?" asked Gram.

"Sydney decided to write a story about her vacation," she said. "I still don't have any idea what to write."

Sydney had slept over at Abby's house the night before. The plan was to work on their stories together. Sydney had started to write hers. But Abby could only think about meeting Abigail Flynn.

Gram winked. "I'm sure you'll think of a great idea," she said.

They passed the sign for Evergreen Nursing Home. Gram turned into the parking lot. They pulled into a parking space and got out of the car.

Abby's heart was beating very fast. "What should I say?" she asked.

"Just tell her where you live," Gram said, putting her arm around Abby. "And show her the key. I'll be right there if you need help."

They asked for Abigail Flynn at the reception desk.

A pretty nurse smiled and pointed down the hallway. "She's in Room 54," she said. "She's still a little tired from her birthday party. But she'll be happy to see you. She doesn't get many visitors."

"Why doesn't she get visitors?" Abby asked.

The nurse leaned down to whisper to Abby, "She's 100 years old, honey! All of her friends have passed away. And she doesn't have any family left, either."

Abby felt sad. She followed the nurse down the hall to Room 54.

Sunlight streamed through the window, making the little yellow room look cheerful and bright. A tiny little woman sat in a wheelchair looking out at a flower garden.

"Abigail," said the nurse, "you have some visitors."

Abigail turned to greet them. Her hair was snowy white and curly. Her blue eyes crinkled at the corners. She held out her hand to Abby. "Hello," she said. "I'm Abigail Flynn."

Abby took her hand. "I'm Abby Spencer," she said. "This is my grandma, Judy Simon."

Abigail's face creased into a sweet smile. She squeezed Abby's hand. "Is your name Abigail, too?" she asked.

Abby nodded. "Yes," she said. "I think I live where your house used to be. My address is 549 Pine Street."

Abigail made a sad little sound. "Oh, Pine Street," she said softly. "What a lovely old house."

"I found a picture of it at the library," said Abby.

Abigail turned her wheelchair toward a small desk in the corner. "I think I still have some pictures of that house on Pine Street. Would you like to see them?" she said.

"Oh, yes!" said Abby.

The first picture was very faded. "The house was yellow with white porches and blue shutters," Abigail pointed out. "You can't tell that from this old picture."

Abby fumbled with the key around her neck. "I think maybe I found the key to your house," she said, holding it out. "My dog dug it up in the yard."

Abigail gasped and put her hand to her mouth. "That's not the house key!" she whispered. "This was the key to my playhouse."

"You had a playhouse?" Abby asked.

Abigail nodded. "My grandfather loved me very much," she said. "He always spoiled me. He built me a beautiful playhouse near the back of the garden."

Abigail's eyes were bright with tears. She slid the key from Abby's fingers and held it against her chest. "My beautiful playhouse," she repeated. "I haven't thought of it in years."

Abby blinked tears away, too. "Do you have any pictures of it?" she asked.

Abigail nodded. "I think I might," she said. She scattered old photographs across the desk. "Here's one! See how beautiful it was?"

Abby took the picture. The playhouse had tall, thin windows and painted shutters. The top of the door was round with a flower carved in the center. Roses tumbled over the stone wall beside it.

Abby's hands started to shake. "Gram," she said, "our old shed was Abigail's playhouse! Daddy and Dakota are going to tear it down today!"

Abby to the Rescue

The drive to Evergreen Nursing Home had seemed to take a long time. The trip home took even longer! Every traffic light turned red just before they got to it.

Abby's foot tapped madly against the floor. "Can't we go any faster?" she asked.

Gram glanced back at Abby. "I can drive faster," Gram said. "But I might get a speeding ticket!"

"What if the shed is gone when we get home?" Abby asked. "What if I can't save it in time?"

"Then we'll tell Abigail the truth. Her playhouse is gone," said Gram. "I don't think she ever dreamed it was still standing."

"But I feel so bad," said Abby. "It didn't burn in the fire that destroyed Abigail's house. But people didn't know what it was when they built new houses on the lots. We just stored paint and tools in it."

"It still needs a lot of work to fix it, Abby," Gram said. "Your father may not want to spend money on it just because it was Abigail's playhouse."

"But it could be my playhouse now!" Abby protested.

"Just remember that your father will have to pay for all the materials," said Gram. "You'll have to let him make the decision whether to tear it down or keep it."

"I know," Abby said in a small voice. "I just hope we get there in time. I need to tell Daddy the whole story."

"I think we'll get there in time," said Gram. "Your father was waiting for the dumpster to come before he began to work."

"But Dakota wanted to start right away," Abby wailed. "I wish you had a cell phone!"

"We'll be home in five minutes," Gram assured her. "Now just relax! Worrying won't change anything."

Abby looked again at the picture she held in her hand. Abigail's playhouse must have been new when the picture had been taken. A little brick walk led up to the playhouse door. Flowers stood in bright rows around it. The door with the round top looked like something out of a fairy tale.

"We have to save it," Abby whispered to herself. "We have to get there in time."

The dumpster was in the driveway when they pulled in. Abby opened the car door and raced to the backyard.

"Slow down!" called Gram.

Abby kept on running. "Stop!" she screamed at the top of her voice. "Stop!"

She raced around the garage and skidded to a stop. The shed stood

untouched in the bright spring sunlight. No one was in sight. "Daddy? Dakota?" Abby called. "Where is everyone?"

The back door to the house opened. "What's the matter?" Abby's mom asked.

Abby rushed toward the house. Then, she saw the wooden ladder lying on the ground. The bottom two rungs were broken.

"Where's Daddy?" Abby asked as her mom came out on the porch. "Did someone get hurt?"

Abby's mom shook her head. "Everyone is fine. Dakota knocked the ladder over. It hit the stone wall on the way down and broke. Daddy had to go buy a new ladder."

Abby sighed in relief. "I'm so glad," she said.

Abby's mom laughed. "You're glad Dakota broke the ladder?"

"No, I'm glad that Daddy didn't start tearing down the shed," Abby answered. She walked up the steps. "Look at this picture. Our shed was Abigail Flynn's playhouse! My key is the key to the front door!"

"I have always loved that door!" said Abby's mom. She looked across the yard at the old shed. "Wouldn't it be nice if we could make it look like new again?"

"Could we?" begged Abby. "Do you think Daddy would fix it for me?"

"I think your dad likes to make you happy," said Abby's mom. "We'll talk about it as soon as he gets back from the hardware store."

"I'm sorry he had to buy a new ladder," said Abby. "Maybe he won't even need one, now!"

"He needed a new ladder," said Abby's mom. "That old wooden one was in the shed when we moved into this house."

Abby laughed. "Maybe it was Abigail's, too!" she said.

Abby's mom laughed. "Maybe it was."

Writer's Block

Abby scrunched up a piece of paper and pushed it to the side of the table. She had started five different stories and she didn't like any of them. She had hoped that coming to the library would help her write, but it hadn't helped at all!

Mrs. Mackenzie walked past with an armful of glittery butterflies to hang in the Children's Area. She patted Abby's shoulder. "What's the matter?" she asked.

Abby sighed. "I shouldn't have signed up for this creative writing contest," she said. "I don't have any good ideas!"

Mrs. Mackenzie put her butterflies carefully on the table and sat down. A little puff of gold glitter floated through the air and landed on Abby's notepad.

"I'm sure you have lots of good ideas," Mrs. Mackenzie said. She pointed to the pile of crumpled pages. "What are all those?"

"Stories that didn't work," Abby said. She looked at all the books on the shelves around her. "I thought if I wrote here at the library, maybe I could think of a good story."

"You don't have to rush," said Mrs. Mackenzie. "The contest deadline is still a week away."

Abby looked down. She ran her finger through the glitter and watched it sparkle in the light. "I know, but Sydney finished her story yesterday," she said quietly. "Everyone else has started their story but me."

"What did Sydney write about?" asked Mrs. Mackenzie.

"Her story is about her vacation last

year," said Abby. "She went to the beach with her family."

"That was a good idea!" said Mrs. Mackenzie. "It's easier to write about things you know."

Abby looked up at Mrs. Mackenzie and grinned. "Then Dakota is going to have a lot of trouble. He's working on a story about pirates and buried treasure!"

Mrs. Mackenzie laughed. She pointed to Abby's necklace. "You have buried treasure of your own," she said.

Abby just stared at Mrs. Mackenzie for a second. Her fingers felt for the key hanging around her neck. "I just had an awesome idea!" she said, jumping up. "I can write about Abigail and her playhouse!"

Mrs. Mackenzie smiled. "Well, there you go! I knew you'd think of something special!"

Abby clapped her hands. "I love this idea!" she said. "I could call it *The Mystery of the Golden Key!*"

"That's a great title!" said Mrs. Mackenzie. She stood up and gathered her butterflies. Glitter drifted onto the floor, making the carpet sparkle and shimmer. "Maybe I better leave you alone so you can write."

"Wait," said Abby. "Can I look at that book about old houses again?"

"Sure," said Mrs. Mackenzie. "I'll get it for you just as soon as I hang up these butterflies."

"I can help!" said Abby. "I feel so much better now that I know what my story will be about!" She did a little happy dance around Mrs. Mackenzie and the butterflies.

Mrs. Mackenzie laughed. "I'll give you a book about Evergreen's early history, too," she said. "You can read all about Abigail's grandfather."

Abby bounced from one foot to another. "This is an awesome idea!" she said. "I don't know why I didn't think about it before! I could even use Abigail's old picture of the playhouse."

Mrs. Mackenzie pulled the ladder over. She handed Abby the butterflies to hold. "How is the work on the playhouse coming?" she asked.

"Daddy is putting a new roof on it today," said Abby. "There was a lot of hammering this morning. I'm not supposed to look. He wants it to be a surprise."

"It would be very hard not to peek," said Mrs. Mackenzie.

"Daddy covered it with a tarp on the side toward the house," said Abby. "He sneaks behind it and then pops back out again."

"It's very exciting," said Mrs. Mackenzie. "Does Miss Flynn know what he's doing?"

Abby nodded. "Gram and I went back to see her again. I told her we had saved her playhouse. I'm so glad we did! I can hardly wait to see it when it is all done."

"I'm glad you saved it, too," said Mrs. Mackenzie. "It's a part of Evergreen's history!"

"And it's going to be a big part of my story, too!" said Abby. "I can't wait to get started!"

And the Winner Is . . .

Do you need some help with the cookie trays?" Abby asked Mrs. Mackenzie. She and Sydney were passing out flyers at the door. The program room was filling up fast. Dakota and Zachary had to set up more chairs.

Mrs. Mackenzie set a huge pitcher of lemonade on the refreshment table. "You kids aren't supposed to be helping!" she protested. "All of the writers are special guests tonight!"

Abby wanted to help. It kept her mind off the contest. "That's okay," she said. "We're your Book Bunch. We like to help!"

Mrs. Mackenzie smiled. "Well, all right. You and Sydney can get the cookie trays if you want to."

"I think half of the third and fourth graders are here tonight," Sydney hissed as they walked into the workroom.

Abby's tummy did a flip-flop. She turned to look at Sydney. "Do you think they all wrote stories?" she asked. "I'll never have a chance of winning!"

Sydney flipped her blonde hair back with her hand. "You don't know that! Mr. Kim always says you are a good writer."

"So are you," said Abby.

Sydney gave her a dazzling smile. "Then maybe there will be a tie and we'll both win!" she said.

Abby giggled. "In your dreams," she said. "Is Mr. Kim here?"

"He came in just as we left the program room," said Sydney. "I saw the mayor, too."

"The mayor came?" Abby gasped. "Why is he here?"

"His grandson is in the fourth grade," Sydney reminded her. "Let's take these cookies out before Mrs. Mackenzie comes looking for us!"

Abby and Sydney each carried a tray. Abby's dad was standing just inside

the program room. He put a finger to his lips. He grabbed a sugar cookie with pink icing and popped it into his mouth.

"Daddy!" Abby protested. "The cookies are for after they announce the winner."

Her dad just laughed. "Come sit with us," he said. "We saved seats for you and Sydney."

Abby put her tray down. Her mom and Sydney's mom were waving. "Let's go and sit down," said Abby. "We can help Mrs. Mackenzie afterward."

"You mean while I'm having my picture taken?" Sydney teased.

Abby laughed. "Yes," she said. "You can be the winner and I'll help Mrs. Mackenzie."

Sydney messed up Abby's hair. Abby untied the ribbon on Sydney's shirt. They both giggled as they ran to sit down.

Mrs. Mackenzie went to the front of the room to start the program. Everyone was talking. Dakota put two fingers in his mouth and whistled. Everyone laughed and then got very quiet.

"Welcome to our first Young Writers' Contest!" said Mrs. Mackenzie. "Submissions were accepted only from members of the third and fourth grade classes at Perry Elementary School. We had fifty-seven entries. Isn't that amazing?"

Everyone clapped.

Mrs. Mackenzie continued. "Now, I would like to introduce Mr. William Jackson, author of the Miss Mayfield Mystery series. He will tell us a little bit about being an author and then announce our winner."

Abby slumped down in her seat. It had taken her three days to write her story. She had made it a beautiful cover with a glittery gold key. She didn't want to have to wait anymore. She just wanted to know who had won.

"Let me show you a picture of my secretary," said Mr. Jackson. "This is Miss Mayfield and she was the inspiration behind my books!" A picture appeared on the screen of his cat sitting at the computer as though she was writing a story. Everyone laughed.

Mr. Jackson pointed at the audience. "Each of you is a storyteller!" he said. "Every day, stories swirl around you just like magic! All you need to do is to catch that magic and write it down!"

Mr. Jackson tapped the stack of manuscripts on the table. "Each of these stories was magical in its own way. But one of our young writers told a story that was not only magical but true."

Abby sat up in her seat. This was it! He was going to announce the winner.

"This writer crafted an exciting mystery with lovable characters and a very happy ending," Mr. Jackson continued. He held up a shiny trophy with a pen and a book on it. "This year's winner of the Young Writers' Contest is Abby Spencer for her story, *The Mystery of the Golden Key*!"

Abby couldn't move. She heard people clapping. Sydney was jumping

up and down beside her. Her dad was thumping her on the back and cheering.

"You won!" Abby's dad said. "Go up front!"

Abby walked to the front of the room. Her heart was pounding and she couldn't stop smiling.

"Congratulations!" said Mr. Jackson as he handed her the trophy.

Cameras flashed! People stood up and clapped!

Abby felt a hand on her shoulder. A little cloud of gold glitter floated down onto the trophy.

"I knew you could do it!" whispered Mrs. Mackenzie.

Happy Endings

"They're here!" Abby yelled as the big white van from Evergreen Nursing Home pulled up outside her house. She grabbed the folder with her story and ran out the door. She could see Abigail Flynn sitting inside the van. Abby waved and jumped up and down.

Abby's parents and Gram gathered to watch as a nurse guided Abigail's wheelchair down the ramp.

Abby grabbed Abigail's hand as soon as she reached the sidewalk. "The playhouse is all finished!" Abby announced with a grin. "Daddy put the shutters on yesterday."

Abigail squeezed Abby's hand. "I'm so excited to see it!" she said. She smiled at Abby's parents. "Thank you so much for inviting me."

"It's our pleasure," said Abby's dad. He glanced at the nurse. "May I take her to the backyard?" he asked, pointing at the wheelchair.

"Of course," said the nurse.

Abby's dad pushed the wheelchair carefully across the grass. Abby ran ahead to stand beside the playhouse. She hopped from one foot to the other. She could hardly wait to see Abigail's expression when she saw it!

Abby's dad pushed the wheelchair around the corner of the house. Abigail's face beamed. "Oh, it's beautiful," she whispered, covering her mouth with her hands. "It looks just the way I remember it."

Abby clapped her hands. "Does it?" she asked. "We tried so hard to make it look like the picture."

Abigail had tears in her eyes. "I'm so glad you decided to paint it yellow with blue shutters," she said. "It used to match my house."

Abby wiggled the key on her necklace. "And guess what?" she asked. "The key still fits! Daddy just had to oil the lock!"

"And you painted the door blue," Abigail said. "It's just perfect!"

Abby pointed at the stone wall. "The old stone wall was still there," she said. "My mom planted two rose bushes beside it, but they aren't blooming yet."

Abigail looked up eagerly. "What color will the roses be?" she asked.

"Pink," said Abby's mom. "I let Abby choose. She liked the pink ones best."

Abigail closed her eyes. "My roses were pink, too," she said. "And they always smelled so sweet."

"The Historical Society came yesterday to take pictures," said Abby's dad. "People we don't even know keep stopping by to see the playhouse! I think we should start serving refreshments!"

"Speaking of refreshments," said Gram, "I'll get some cookies and lemonade. We can all sit out here and admire the playhouse."

"Thank you all so much," Abigail said. "I feel as though I got a little bit of my childhood back!"

Abby's dad smiled. "I like to have a project," he said. "It makes me forget about work for a while."

Mr. and Mrs. Spencer arranged lawn chairs around Abigail's wheelchair.

Lucy escaped when Gram came out with the cookies. She gave Abigail a slobbery kiss and ran off to chase shadows across the yard.

Abigail turned to Abby. "I saw your picture in the paper!" she said. "Congratulations on winning the creative writing contest, dear! I would love to hear your story sometime."

Abby grinned. "I made a copy for you to keep!" Abby took her story out of the folder. The gold key on the front sparkled and glittered as she handed it to Abigail.

"Oh, it's beautiful!" said Abigail. She patted the chair beside her. "Would you read it to me now?"

Abby sat down beside her and turned to the first page. Stray bits of glitter twinkled on the white paper as they caught the sunlight. Abby smiled. Maybe Mr. Jackson was right. Maybe stories were made of magic!

The Mystery of the Golden Key

by:

Abby Spencer

The Mystery of the Golden Key

by Abby Spencer

On the first day of spring break, something very exciting happened! My dog, Lucy, dug up a golden chain with a golden key in my front yard!

The key looked very old. It had a heart with the letter A inside. My name, Abby, begins with A. It seemed like that key was made just for me!

I showed the key to my mom and dad. Daddy said it was a house key, but it didn't belong to our house. My friend Dakota thought it might open a pirate chest. The key was a mystery!

Daddy took us to the library to see what we could find out about old keys. But Mrs. Mackenzie gave us a book about old houses instead.

She looked up my address. There was a picture of a beautiful house at my address. But it wasn't my house. The house belonged to George Flynn. It burned down in 1937.

Mr. Flynn's granddaughter lived in the house, too. Her name was Abigail! I thought maybe the key belonged to her. I wished that I could find out for sure.

Then, Gram found a picture of Abigail Flynn in the newspaper. She is 100 years old! She lives at Evergreen Nursing Home. Gram took me to visit her.

I showed Abigail my key. She said it was the key to the playhouse she had when she was a little girl! Abigail had an old picture of her playhouse. It looked a lot like the shed behind my house!

I was worried. Daddy wanted to tear the shed down because it was old. I showed him the picture of Abigail's playhouse. I asked him if he could fix it up as a playhouse for me. He said, "Yes!"

Now the playhouse is beautiful again! It is yellow with blue shutters and a blue door. It has pink roses growing around it. The golden key still fits the lock!

Now I have a new playhouse and a new friend named Abigail Flynn. I'm so happy we solved the mystery of the golden key!!

You Can Be an Author, Too!

You have to use your writing skills every day at school, but you can also write for fun! Here are some ideas to try:

• Start a journal or a diary. Write down the important things that happen to you or any thoughts you want to remember each day.

• Start with a familiar story, like a fairy tale, and add some new characters. Write a new ending or beginning for it.

• Make up a strange new kind of animal with a funny name. Write a story about its adventures.

• Write an adventure story about your favorite character from a game or television show.

• Write a story about your pet or a family member.